First published in the United States
of America in 1990 by The Mallard Press

Mallard Press and its accompanying design
and logo are trademarks of BDD Promotional
Book Company, Inc.

Produced by
Twin Books
15 Sherwood Place
Greenwich, CT 06830

ISBN 0 792 45406 5

Printed in Hong Kong

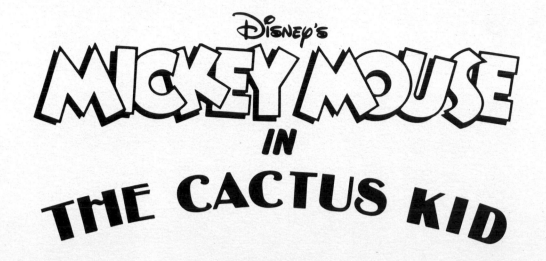

DISNEY'S
MICKEY MOUSE
IN
THE CACTUS KID

Written by
Lee Nordling

TWIN BOOKS

MALLARD
PRESS

Mickey Mouse and Minnie stepped off the train. From the depot, the town of Sagebrush looked a hundred years old.

"Oh, Mickey," said Minnie. "This is going to be a wonderful Western vacation! Where's Goofy?"

"Here I am!" said Goofy, getting off the train in his brand-new, cowboy-style clothes. "I wanted to change before anyone mistook me for one of them tenderfeet!"

An old man with a wide moustache approached them with open arms. "Mickey, Minnie! I'm glad you could make it."

"Thanks for inviting us," said Mickey. "Handlebar Harry, I'd like you to meet my friend, Goofy."

Goofy stuck out his hand and said, "Howdy, pardner."

Mickey, Minnie and Goofy piled their bags into the back of Harry's wagon, and the four of them headed for Harry's ranch, the Bar None.

"Gawrsh!" said Goofy. "This is just like the Old West!"

"Yup," answered Harry. "We even have cattle rustlers."

"Rustlers?" said Mickey and Minnie.

"I'm afraid so," said Harry. "They've just about run me out of business. I think my neighbor, Pecos Pete, is behind the rustling, but I've never been able to prove it. I need your help, Mickey."

"What can we do to help?" said Mickey while they waited in their wagon for some cowboys to move cattle across the road.

Harry said, "See that steer? That's Old Snorty. He should have my Bar None brand on him, but he doesn't. He's wearing Pecos Pete's Double Diamond brand, so I can't prove he's really mine."

Harry paused and thought about what he'd just said. Then he started hopping up and down as if he'd sat on an ant hill. "Stop, you rustlers!" he shouted. "Those are my cattle!"

Pecos Pete rode up. "Well, well!" he said. "If it isn't my old pals!"

"We're not your pals!" said Mickey. "And you'd better give Harry back the cattle you stole, or I'm going to do something about it!"

Pete reached over, grabbed Mickey, and said, "Listen, pip-squeak! You won't do anything about anything! And if you don't keep your nose out of my business, something real bad might happen to Harry. Get it?"

Pete spun his horse around and rode after his gang of rustlers, laughing all the way.

Handlebar Harry was still angry when they got to the Bar None. "If I were thirty years younger, I'd show that Pecos Pete a thing or two!" He slumped into an overstuffed chair and added, "But the Cactus Kid will never ride again."

"Who's the Cactus Kid?" asked Mickey.

"I am. Or *was*," said Harry. He pointed to a bright green Western outfit hanging in a display case. "I fought for truth, justice, and every little guy that needed help. Now, I can't even help myself."

Goofy puffed out his chest and said, "I'll help! You just aim me at those rustlers and I'll take off like a speeding bullet!"

As Goofy ran out to saddle a horse, Handlebar Harry tried to slow him down. "Goofy, I'm not sure you know what you're getting into. Pecos Pete and his gang are pretty tough!"

"I've met his kind before," said Goofy as he hopped on his horse. "And my luck is bound to improve!"

Goofy trotted out the gate, so intent on his mission that he didn't notice he was sitting backwards on his horse. Harry's ranch hands laughed and laughed, but Harry was worried.

Mickey watched from a window and made a decision.

Minnie joined Mickey at the window. "Do you want to pack a picnic basket and go for a ride?" she asked. "Maybe we can catch up with Goofy."

"No thanks, Minnie," said Mickey. "I think I'll take a nap."

This surprised Minnie. She had been certain Mickey would want to keep an eye on Goofy. However, she went ahead and packed a picnic, saddled up and headed for the open range.

It wasn't long before she found Goofy helping a band of masked men herd Handlebar Harry's cattle.

"Goofy, what are you doing?" asked Minnie.

"That's funny," said Goofy. "When I met these fellows I asked them the same thing. I thought they might be rustlers. But they told me they weren't. They're hiding Harry's cattle so they won't be stolen. They're even letting me help."

Minnie said, "Goofy, these men *are* rustlers. They lied to you."

"You did?" said Goofy to the rustlers. They all nodded their heads and said, "Yep."

"Gawrsh, Minnie!" said Goofy. "It looks like these beeswaxers have got our goose up a tree!"

Minnie sighed. "That's *bushwhackers,* and it's a cat up a tree, not a goose. *Our* goose is *cooked.*

"Anyway, it's the end of the trail, said Goofy.

Then a blaze of green lightning and leather streaked down the hill. It was the Cactus Kid riding a wild black stallion. The Kid twirled two lassos over his head.

The rustlers gasped at the sight of the Cactus Kid. They turned and galloped away with the Kid in hot pursuit.

"Who was that green masked man?" wondered Goofy.

When Minnie and Goofy returned to the ranch, they told Handlebar Harry about the strange masked man who had saved the cattle.

"What did he look like?" asked Mickey as he walked into the room, yawning.

"That's him!" said Goofy. He pointed to the Cactus Kid costume inside the display case and said, "At least, that's the outside part. Underneath, he was big, and strong, and fearless. Sort of like me."

"It sounds like there's a *new* Cactus Kid," said Harry.

There *was* a new Cactus Kid! Over the next several weeks he raised a storm of justice across the entire valley. Pecos Pete and his rustlers were foiled at every turn.

When they tried to ford a river with their stolen cattle, the Kid was there to stop them. When they tried to cross the sands, the Kid seemed to leap out of the blazing sun to drive them back. When they tried to sneak through the mountain passes, the Cactus Kid and his horse, Twister, were always there to head them off.

The Cactus Kid was becoming a legend again!

Pecos Pete stomped on the latest edition of the local paper, *The Sagebrush Star*. "The Cactus Kid! The Cactus Kid!" he raged. "That's all I read about! 'Cactus Kid Saves Valley.' 'Cactus Kid Stops Rustlers.' 'Cactus Kid a Hero.'"

Pete grabbed one of his gang members by the coat and snarled, "Why don't they print *my* side? 'Rustlers Out of Work.' 'Rustlers Embarrassed.' 'Rustlers Shed Tear for Good Old Days!'"

Pete smashed his fist through the wall. "I want to find out who the Cactus Kid really is and I want him stopped! Get me?"

Meanwhile, at the Sagebrush Saloon, Goofy was retelling a story that got better with each telling. "And there I was," said Goofy to the card players, "trapped like a prairie rat in a mine shaft, rustlers all around me! But was I scared?" The men nodded.

"No," continued Goofy. "I reached out, grabbed them by the scruff of their necks and shook their boots off!"

"When did the Cactus Kid save you?" asked one of the cowboys.

"Who?" said Goofy. "Oh, *him*. Well..."

"I think Goofy's pulling our legs," said another man with a wink. "I think *he's* really the Cactus Kid."

"I'm not saying I am," said Goofy, "and I'm not saying I'm not." All the men laughed, except one. He was Pecos Pete's spy. And he soon rushed off to tell Pete the news.

31

When Goofy got back to the Bar None, Minne was waiting. "Come on, Goofy," she called. "We're taking Mickey for a ride. He hasn't been out of the house since we got here."

"Sure thing, Minnie," said Goofy as he hopped on the buckboard. "Don't you worry, Mickey. I'll protect you!"

They rode out to the wide-open spaces of Harry's ranch. Minnie said, "Isn't this exciting, Mickey? Mickey, wake up!"

Mickey woke from his nap, looked around and said, "*Too* exciting! Who invited them?" Minnie and Goofy turned around and saw a dozen rustlers charging toward them.

Pecos Pete and his rustlers surrounded the buckboard.
Pete growled, "Okay, Kid! You're coming with us!"

Mickey sighed and started to get down, but Pete said, "Not you, pip-squeak!" He pointed to Goofy and said, "You! The Cactus Kid!"

"Who, me?" said Goofy. The rustlers nodded. Goofy stuck his hands up and stepped down.

Pete bound and gagged Goofy, put him on a horse and rode off.

"We can't follow them in this buckboard," said Mickey. "Let's get back to the ranch!"

"I have an idea," said Mickey.

Soon Minnie, Harry and all the ranch hands knew that it was Mickey who had been acting as the Cactus Kid. He called them together to explain his plan.

"Now that Pete thinks he's captured the Cactus Kid, he'll go on a rustling rampage!" said Mickey. "And we're going to trap him!"

He pointed to a large pyramid of paint cans and said, "Over the last few days, I've bought every can of glow-in-the-dark paint in Sagebrush. Now, I need your help to stop Pecos Pete and save Harry's ranch. Are you with me?" The ranch hands raised a cheer.

Later that afternoon, Pecos Pete and his rustlers found all of Handlebar Harry's cattle grazing in a pasture. No one was in sight. But as soon as the rustlers started rounding up the cattle, Mickey and the ranch hands sprang their trap. They snagged the thieves with lassos and pulled them from their saddles.

Pecos Pete dodged two lassos and cracked his whip to stampede the cattle. As the cattle started to run, Pete escaped with the frightened animals. He had stolen all of Harry's cattle.

Mickey called out to Harry. "Did we get them all?"

"All except Pete!" said Harry.

"Don't worry about Pete," said Mickey. He turned Twister around and galloped off.

Pete relaxed by his campfire and looked at Goofy. "So, you weren't the Cactus Kid after all," he said.

"Murphlelumptilumpas," said Goofy, still gagged.

"You're right, it is a beautiful evening," agreed Pete.

"And it's the last one you're going to see without bars," said Mickey as he lassoed Pete.

"You've got nothing on me!" said Pete. "These cattle are carrying *my* brand, not Harry's!"

"That's where you're wrong," said Mickey. He stomped out the campfire. By the light of the moon, Pete and Goofy could clearly see the Bar None brand on the cattle, highlighted with glow-in-the-dark paint. "Now anyone call tell how you've been changing the brand," Mickey said. "Your rustling days are over!"

The next day, Handlebar Harry had a big party at his ranch. Finally he asked Mickey, "Why did you pretend to be the Cactus Kid?"

"I think I know," said Minnie. "Pete had threatened you if Mickey didn't stay out of the way. Mickey decided to wear a disguise, so Pete wouldn't harm you. And it worked."

"It sure did," said Harry with a wink. "For a while there, even I thought Goofy was the Cactus Kid."

Goofy said, "Me, too!" And everyone laughed.